What Are You?

Words by **Christian Trimmer**
Art by **Mike Curato**

Roaring Brook Press

New York

Arranging
flowers

and watching
cartoons

and practicing
yoga

and eating
cupcakes

and
break dancing

and doing this
with my tongue

and composing
symphonies

and speaking
French!

I am good at those things because I like them and I practice and I am me.

And I am good at those things because I like them and I practice and I am me!

and doing
cartwheels

and singing
show tunes

and solving
college-level mathematics

and speaking
French!

Tips for Caregivers

What Are You? is a playful story about three dogs that touches on bigger themes such as identity, families, and stereotypes. Welcome and encourage conversations about race and culture with children. These early discussions weave the fabric of inclusivity, acceptance, and mutual respect for others.

• Reflect on your child's day-to-day observations about others in a nonjudgmental way. Use their natural observations as teachable moments.

  "You noticed that Edward's parents have different skin colors."

• Respond to inaccurate statements from children with curiosity. They might come from misunderstanding or misinformation.

  "Tell me more about what you mean by 'parents are supposed to look the same.'"

• Correct inaccurate statements and challenge stereotypes with patience and without shame.

  "Some people have darker skin and some people have lighter skin. Just as hair can come in different colors and textures, skin can look different too. And people who look different can love each other and be in a family together."

• Use empathy to tackle discussions about racism and discrimination. Focus on fairness/unfairness. Imagine how certain actions might make someone feel.

Conversation Starters

- How are the three dogs the same? How are they different?

- What are some ways that you are the same or different from other children you know who don't look or speak like you?

- Sometimes family members look different from one another. What are some ways that family members can be the same or different?

- Why do you think the two poodles believed that all pugs are good at Hula-Hoop?

- Sometimes people think that "all boys" or "all girls" like or do the same kinds of things. Share some examples that prove this wrong. What are other ways that individuals from the same group might actually be very different from each other?

- What are some assumptions others have made about you that have been wrong?

- What are some examples of things we cannot know about a person just by looking at them?

- What are some ways that we can better get to know people who may be different from ourselves?

Tips and conversation starters written by Dr. Danielle Vrieze, PhD, LP, child psychologist and assistant professor at the University of Minnesota Medical School.

To Mom and Dad, for creating me,

and Britton and Nicole, for understanding me

—C. T.

For Katrina and Kyle—

What are you . . . laughing at?

—M. C.

Published by Roaring Brook Press

Roaring Brook Press is a division of Holtzbrinck Publishing Holdings Limited Partnership

120 Broadway, New York, NY 10271 ⋆ mackids.com

Text copyright © 2022 by Christian Trimmer. Illustrations copyright © 2022 by Mike Curato.
All rights reserved.

Our books may be purchased in bulk for promotional, educational, or business use.
Please contact your local bookseller or the Macmillan Corporate and Premium Sales Department at
(800) 221-7945 ext. 5442 or by email at MacmillanSpecialMarkets@macmillan.com.

Library of Congress Cataloging-in-Publication Data is available.

First edition, 2022

The illustrations in this book were created digitally with Procreate, and the text was set in CC Extra Extra.
The book was edited by Jennifer Besser and art directed by Lisa Vega. The production editor was Mia Moran,
and the production was managed by Allene Cassagnol.

Printed in China by RR Donnelley Asia Printing Solutions Ltd., Dongguan City, Guangdong Province

ISBN 978-1-250-78602-9

1 3 5 7 9 10 8 6 4 2